the knight shall not come

a story of a -r-o-y-a-l- broken family

Harshini Sre Palanivenkatcsan

ISBN 9798897771271

for,

all the teens,

who's eyes search for words,

and maybe,

m

a

y

b

e

want to be,

a paper girl in a paper world

(princess of light)

you remember,

 six-year-old you,

grooving to indian beats,

lock and key- with your cousins,

in the land of history,

of colour,

(also, a land lacking in so many ways,

you couldn't,

c o m p r e h e n d)

your mom and dad,

well versed,

in a group of average,

(**average** *like you,*

you thought)

wanted a future,

beyond the soil,

that had fed their dreams,

b e f o r e

they wanted a life of plenty

in the land of dreams,

the

american

dream,

(spoiler i. not a dream after all)

they typed,

all they seemed to do,

the blisters on your palms,

from monkey bars,

should have been,

w o r s e,

on their fingertips,

you thought.

you remember,

the sharp shoot of pain,

when they told you,

we're moving far,

far away…

you remember

tears and hugs,

the knight shall not come   5

all your favourite foods,

on the last day,

before the witchcraft,

took you over the waves,

you remember,

 feeling so **out of place,**

 in kindergarten,

where children rambled a language,

 you thought you knew,

but twisted the words,

 into scribbles on a page,

playgrounds,

and big apartments,

shiny new bikes,

and soon,

words tumbled out of you,

            in the same "colourful" way,

                              – indian girls in "dreamland"

(princess of dark)

(definition. *out of place*

phrase of place

not in the proper position; disarranged.

alia, i.e. me)

– definitions that hurt

(princess of light)

at 7, a little doll, with miniature toes,

(mira, you said)

made itself at home,

one-bedroom apartment,

house filled with laughter,

and the bare walls,

empty rooms felt like home,

peekaboo's,

rattles littered on the carpet,

smiling without teeth,

a place in your heart,

at 8, it tattered on,

repeating your name,

almost on its feet,

flaying its arms,

 as it babbled,

'ali' 'ali',

(alia, but who cares anyway?)

 it cried,

making it's way into your arms,

you were,

home from school,

tired but excited

mom stayed at home,

new person,

no worries?

l
i
s
t
e
n
i
n
g

the paintings,

you laid out,

with words,

towering above you,

a smile,

at your sister's mischief,

"good night,"

she said,

laying you to bed,

a bedtime kiss,

sweet dreams

and recess,

filling up your mind,

yet,

 there's something about your skin color,

your glasses,

your raised hand in class,

your witty answers,

(they make you invisible)

your bindi and your smelly rice,

that makes them steer away,

the way your mom's english,

thick with an accent,

the way she wears kurtis to work,

and though they stare,

(they make you invisible)

to everyone but your teachers,

they stare in

a m a z e m e n t

the calculations,

you do on your mind,

others counting out on fingers,

everyone,

but a pale girl,

with skin,

 white as the moon,

(who you stare at in wonder, why don't you look
like that?)

beside you,

her hand raised up,

sitting in kumon,

speed through sums,

on the green grass,

looking for lucky clovers,

at swimming,

both learn to paddle,

you smile at each other,

exchanging few words,

because you don't know

english as well as the others,

but you see her

you're meant to be friends,

 handshakes and secrets,

exchanged over recess,

 and later,

you pour over your homework,

 teaching each other,

gossiping and girly,

(almost like the others.)

new dresses,

haircuts,

all the latest fashion,

you try to fit in,

but you're both like

d a n d e l i o n s

in

a

field

of

r o s e s.

        – who said roses are better than dandelions?

(the queen)

(spoiler ii.
"treat me like a queen,
and i'll treat you like a king,
treat me like a game,
and i'll show you,
how it's played"
or maybe not.)

i was never one of those wives

 who took care of it all,

earned money,

cleaned the dishes,

cared for the children,

i was always the wife whose husband

came home at 5,

(so did i)

and we'd pick them up,

from afterschool,

take them to the park,

do homework,

play with them,

 listen to their every whim,

sure we fought,

but who doesn't with their spouse,

it never lasted days and nights,

 it was for the moment,

the moment only,

why do i keep going back to moments?

"looking bossy," he chuckled,
as i tightened the new work outfit,
i'd bought the other day,

                                    i smiled,
                        "i'm not the bossy one,
                            mira says you are"
"mom only shows her bad side at office,"
he chuckles again,

    "i need to catch a flight! can you drop me or not!"
                        i say pretending to be angry,

"mom shows her bossy side with daddy as well."
i laugh.

everything changes in a moment,
sunny skies to thundering rain,
caring to couldn't care less,
happiness to a shoot of pain,
and silence so loud it deafens,

i always remember,

the back of my mind,

the orphanage,

my silence,

knowing that whatever,

i said   i wanted
even screamt

would not be heard,

it would be a voice in many,

unimportant, uncared for,

ignored.

i studied though,

textbooks an escape,

it was a path to a dream,

envisioned so often,

an engineer,

i thought,

that's where alia,

gets her drive,

(i used to say)

proudly to him,

when he came,
it excited me,
and he cared,
cared so hard,
i forgot the years before it.

that was something i promised myself,
my kids,
it would be unknown to them,
being ignored
f o r e i g n
the accent on my tongue,
they would never feel so lost,
always be heard,
always be seen,

there's something about promises,

you can never keep them,

and i left alia alone,

and i suppose i forgot mira,

i tried to forget her.

       – you're a queen (or a king) period.

(princess of dark)

being brown

in a country so white,

it makes you,

 doubt your every move,

your every word

your every joke,

the smelly food you bring,

the bindi on your forehead,

makes me wish i was american

t h r o u g h

and

t h r o u g h,

mom always tells me,

you're so much more than the religion you follow,

the food you eat,

you're the person who loves her baby sister,

more than her mom could ever,

you're smart and confident,

kind and caring,

your culture is what made you, you,

don't sweep it under the carpet,

like it's a dirty mistake.

i'm the girl,

who doesn't wear flashy dresses,

tight at the hips,

short, below the knee

i'm the girl,

wearing an oversized tee,

and a baggy pair of sweatpants,

not even jeans,

why do i want to be her,

the girls flashing the crop tops,

bikini straps,

why does *showing me off,*

be the only way to fit in?

(will that be me someday?

#do you girl!)

mira danced into the field of white roses,

like she was yellow,

 s p e c i a l,

special not different,

she fits in,

t-shirt with sequins,

rather than the plain old boring ones,

and that fills me with joy,

but also longing,

j e a l o u s y

(why can't i act like that?

why can't i be the class clown?

the funny smart one,

the one that everyone befriends)

mira was the one,

mom let free,

seven-year-old her,

wearing

crop tops,

jeans,

more fashionable than

seventeen-year-old me,

the knight shall not come   23

i remember mira at 4,

i was in my room,

the periodic table,

everything else was easy,

but chemistry so not,

i remember going to the kitchen,

when i felt hungry,

and there she stood,

standing on a chair,

a box full of mangoes on the counter,

and she took a big ripe one,

and started nibbling at the very edge,

"mom," i said, "look at mira",

and she came,

i stood there with a secret smile,

when did mom come,

when i called her?

she never did,

she was always,

 huddled behind the computer,

an awful posture,

 a stressed look on her face,

that day she came,

and she laughed,

a laugh so pure

j   o   y   f   u   l

and i couldn't help but think,

maybe mira would be the one,

to smooth over the cracks.

– your ethnicity is never the
most important part of you.
#browninucountrysowhite

(princess of light)

you lay in bed,

toss and turn,

 waiting for a **miracle**,

you want her back,

clean up the broken glass,

in the family's living room,

 the silence that echoes,

you want her mischief,

you want her lies,

don't sleep till past midnight,

wake at dawn,

carry yourself out of bed,

face the sharp shards downstairs,

sometimes,

when your eyes see her grin,

your ears hear her laughter,

sometimes,

when you can't bear the silence,

hear your thoughts echo through home,

sometimes,

when you see that look from your mother,

the look of pain and anger,

when they don't dare to speak her name,

and she's lost,

you can't sleep,

when you toss and turn,

waiting for a miracle,

(you'll open that sock drawer, ruffling to the
bottom,

and ease the pain.)

sometimes,

when the house is quiet and empty,

a house filled with pink and orange,

now with blue and purple,

the colours of dirty bruises,

sometimes,

when there's silence so loud at the table,

it creeps into your chest and throat,

deafening,

a rock in your throat,

the knight shall not come   27

or maybe your heart,

nothing comes out,

sometime when the only words

 exchanged are those,

'p a s s   t h e   i d l y'

's w i t c h   o n   t h e   h e a t e r',

and the words contain so little,

they contain so much,

that's when you see her in bone and flesh,

a girl with features,

long hair,

brown eyes,

lanky frame,

like her,

your little doll,

mira.

(me)

she talks to you

(almost)

as s p e c i a l

and meaningful

as before,

whispers of her voice,

sound waves

through the still air,

those are the days,

 you sleep almost soundly,

you wake up with a smile,

wash your face,

grab your bag,

walk downstairs,

saying 'g o o d   m o r n i n g',

to father and mother,

 that look up at you and nod,

(they don't look like they

hate you,

just pain

settled over them

a storm,

you're the eye of the storm)

the knight shall not come   29

they try to smile,

(but the smile

 doesn't reach their eyes)

tears to your eyes,

hastily wiping them away,

(think about mira,

sitting upstairs,

with a book in her hand,

doodling,

plotting pranks,

and you're heart settles,

down

and down

and down

its not in your throat,

but it's in your stomach now)

but,

it's funny how she's so young,

but her eyes,

carry all the tears yours could,

her heart feels heavy,

but she holds it all in,

(better than you ever could)

shut up,

you say to the thoughts in your head,

echoing her name endlessly,

she's there upstairs isn't she?

at least she's back,

you tell yourself.

ignore the fact,

she probably cries herself to sleep,

looks down at you sad,

                (and there's something about her,

                        that's not mira.)

she's here,

you repeat

a g a i n

and

a g a i n.

– sometimes people are here but they are n o t

(royal acquaintance)

i remember sitting outside in recess,

(the sharp sting,

being socially awkward)

the next day was the one,

                    i met alia,

she'd flown,

all the way,

heart of delhi,

and she was just like me,

not in a bad way,

but i saw it in her eyes,

immigrant blood,

the blood,

d e s p i s e d,

'hello' she said,

entered the class,

'i am alia' she said,

rough and patchy,

like her country,

her words,

came out all wrong,

she smiled and nodded,

responded, raised her hand,

and she was p r e t t y,

the jealous kids won't admit it,

but her black silky hair radiated,

and her tan complex brought images,

of sunny days laying on the beach,

the sun that doesn't burn,

the sun that casts light above you,

warming your soul,

at recess that day,

'you look so pretty,"

she said to me,

       "wanna be friends?'

         i said to her,

        that was the first time,

           someone

acknowledged

me

she jumped,
 on the monkey bars,
desperately fell off,
i laughed,
stood up,
swinged across,
said,
"that's how you do it!'
she laughed,
a good sport.

silly conversations

 became
 those
about
parents,

those

about

the

weight

of

their

non-existence,

i remember her saying,

after mira was gone,

"i think they hate me,

they ignore me,"

she cried that day,

i held her hand as she cried,

her tears flowing a river,

i wished i could be like that,

cry my heart out,

but i don't want to burden her,

when she's so

burdened,

(sometimes i feel like i have to be that girl,

mira, effortlessly held alia together

sometimes i feel like i have to be the glue,

to fix all the broken parts,

even if i am broken myself.)

– the things you do for your friends

(royal acquaintance pt ii)

at home life hurts even more,

my mother goes,
what are you going to do,
in life getting 80's?
did i bring you here to score like that?
so that you could be average?

                         i stand their silently,
                     shaking my head slowly
                      i'll do better ma , i say,
                        and she stares at me,
              pulls me by me ear through the hall,
                     and locks me in the room.

study, she says from the other end,
and i stand at the closed door crying,
carrying my report card in one hand,
holding my bruised arm in the other,

look at alia, she says to dig it in,

your friend,

throws

that word

meaninglessly,

and i know i shouldn't feel like this,

but for that moment,

i feel like alia should do better,

be a better friend,

i'm there for her,

(why can't i let her,

be there for me?

maybe there's a problem,

with me)

is it that my worries feel small,

in front of hers

am i insensitive?

mira…

i tell myself….

or was it always like this?

was she always the one,

who towered over me,

or is it just that,

 she's the smart one,

she's the pretty one,

mira…

i tell myself….

it's

not

alia

ma

hurts

my

heart,

i've had enough,

 i talk back,

and that's when

there's a sharp sting,

not only the sting of pain,

the sting of a belt,

on my back,

but the sting of regret,

longing,

it's almost as though she has two sides,

with family and friends,

she says,

"my daughter goes to kumon, swims and scores,"

she says,

"i'm sure your child will do better"

lightly holding my hand,

she puts up this whole facade,

i'm a genius student,

i'm a child prodigy,

i'm going to be class valedictorian,

no mom i'm not,

when will i ever be enough for you?

– don't you dare say my mom loves me.

(the princess of dark)

we were up at 6:30,

our friends at 7,

the extra time,

used for prayers,

and white and red powder.

spread on our forehead,

i remember,

lighting the lamps,

burning my fingers,

once or twice,

believing,

 praying,

for all the dogs,

the poor people,

the sad souls,

out there that needed help,

the extra time,

was also used for combing,

my long hair into plaids,

extravagant hairdos,

that no one paid attention to,

oiling my hair with a thick layer,

of coconut oil,

"it'll grow long and strong,"

ma and pa said,

as i complained,

for the umpteenth time,

i didn't care about long,

or strong hair,

as long as people wouldn't,

stare, pinch their nose at,

the smell of the grease,

move their heads away,

from mine,

scared that it would

coat their head

like it does mine,

school was school,

but i craved for one,

other brown skin,

black hair,

the knight shall not come   43

bindi on forehead,

to be seen,

in the sea,

brown curly hair,

brunettes, blond,

red haired even,

white, pink skin

we'd stay late,

with an ocean of

chinese boys and girls,

a white girl,

who's mom,

drove in a motorcycle,

and in after school,

pinkish, orange skin,

she was the,

odd one out.

we'd stay doing crafts,

art, math even,

whiling away time,

till we could go home,

to our traditions,

and family,

despised but also craved.

that was routine.

(definition. ***odd one out***

phrase of <u>place</u>

1. not in the proper position; disarranged.

2. *usually me, sometimes not.*)

– indian girl routine

(the queen)

(spoiler alert iii.

i love a good cookie)

i remember that day,

i looked out the window

mira and alia jumped off the bus,

and shoved the door open,

'you have a birthday today"

i said 'i got a call'

they exchanged a sneaky smile,

'yeah,' nodded mira,

nodding, 'what are you getting her?'

'i never really liked her', said alia

'yeah it's that girl," i say

anastasia was quite the bully,

she targeted mira,

i'm guessing her mom,

 made her invite the class,

or she invited mira,
 to make jokes with,
funny cause mira's the one,
 the class clown
and i know for a fact,
the class loves her,
i wouldn't say in front of my girls,
but
bratty
 anastasia
 is
jealous

        'mhmm, i'm gonna bake her,
            my signature,
         peanut oatmeal raisin cookies"

"save some for us,"
i smile, and instantly crave it,

"wait, you're going to her party?"

alia turned to mira.

"nah, we'll just go and give the cookies,

i have dance practice."

"free cake, mira" i frenzy my hands,

certainly weirdly,

my daughter bakes a cake,

every other day,

she really doesn't need more sugar,

i still say it,

isn't that what mothers,

 are supposed to do,

keep your children in parties,

make them have fun?

(or maybe make them confident enough,

to roast a bully?)

"na don't go to that brats party,"

loudly,

"alia, politely please."

"ma, ask anastasia to be polite"

mira did not go,

she did however,

i n n o c e n t l y,

or so i should think,

place a carton of frosted cookies,

baked with alia's help

on anastasia's doorstep,

except i know for a fact,

from the birthday girl,

being absent for the next few days,

that she was suffering,

from a case of diarrhea.

i never told my girls,

that i was certain,

it was them.

– success is not the sweetest revenge, when
people are   j e a l o u s

(princess of light)

you lay in bed with tears,

your face buried in pillows,

an ocean flowed out of your eyes,

and i couldn't help but cry,

myself,

and the next day,

you stayed at home,

crying till you were numb,

until finally you had enough,

you took out,

a science textbook,

poured yourself into it,

but you repeated the words,

again and again,

nothing seemed to stick,

you were reading it,

to numb the pain

at a small but homely building,

windows showing views,

of colourful classrooms,

sadistic highschoolers,

and teachers,

who seemed to have enough of it all,

a place you would call your second home,

now meaningless in your heart,

you remember walking in,

and you almost felt like all eyes were on you,

and yet they didn't stare,

at the socially awkward,

yet confident young women,

who'd turned into a walking shadow,

elaine waited,

she waited outside as tears flowed in the bathroom,

she waited at the lunch table,

through your murmurs,

of sadness,

she waited for words to fall out of your mouth,

waited for you to return to normal,

and until,

cameron saw you,

(a once sweet boy

on the wrong track)

he handed you a bag,

filled with

p

l

a

s

t

i

c

p

i

l

l

s

(shush!)

you stared him in the eye,

your soul begged to refuse,

your hands betrayed you,

you didn't know the direction,

you were heading for,

> – don't do drugs kid. period (2nd time).

(princess of dark)

"are you coming to the festival?"

i drop my bag on mira's bed,

and look for her in the closet,

she comes out with a smile,

"how can i? you should go,"

she holds her journal in her hand,

"let me see," i say grabbing it,

"hey!"

i look through the last picture,

a picture of a family,

at least what she thinks is a family,

me,

mom

and

dad,

*(**spoiler iii**. dad?)*

except she's missing from the picture,

"why aren't you here?" i ask,

she smiles sadly but doesn't reply,

"oh you're doing it from your perspective,"

i say, "you're looking at us."

"yeah, i guess," enthusiastically,

"now the festival?

ma's making aloo paratha,"

i tease.

"mhmm... bring me some up,"

"i will, when do i not?"

"won't you eat?" she asks,

"don't feel like it."

i feel dumb as i talk to her,

it's almost like she knows,

something i don't,

i don't care,

she's back and that's all that matters.

i'm still holding the journal,

i flip to the first page,

"pretty pranks i've done"

she's written in crayon,

a list of the most basic,

but funny things she's done,

accompanies,

sticking this flashy black sheet,

on mom's computer,

"she thought it was dead, remember?" i say,

the whole april fools prank on dad,

a clean teeth freak,

who brushed with sugar cream,

instead of toothpaste,

        "remember how he screamed at us?"

"yeah but we were laughing so hard,"

        "he started laughing in the end too"

           she exclaims,

the next page is filled with a list,

i don't recognise,

from school,

to the next-door neighbour,

there's elaborate plans,

"there's one on me?" i say,

          "you were studying too hard," she smiles,

               "so worried about college!"

"well now i'm not,"

          "you should be," she nods seriously,

          "actually, go work on your ap classes

               i'll be fine, now"

               *(*cringe*)*

"why now and not then?" i say.

"cause, i'm your imagination now,"

"totally!" i laugh;
but the laugh stays stuck in my throat.

— imaginary girls trying to save a damsel in
distress

(princess of light)

(meaning. damsel in distress

phrase of damsel

1. humorous

a young woman in trouble.

"she makes a rather sweet damsel in distress")

spoiler iv. save yourself.

queen

the bell rings and i open it,

"hey, camila" i say,

"it's been a long time since we met!"

she waddles her way into the house,

"where little alia," she asks?

"not so little anymore!

i fake joy in my tone,

i'm worried about my daughter,

the way she isolates herself,

like she deserves to be in prison,

"anyway, what's up?" i ask,

it's been a long time since i've seen,

the apartment people,

celebrations and festivals,

things i passed,

and no one really asked,

"well we're having a potluck for divali,"

"diwali?" i ask,
"i mean, yeah, a lot of you indians are here,
we thought, why not enjoy your flavors?"

"you better make enchiladas!" i say,
fake joy.
(but almost excited)

"you better make those hot paratas,"
she pronounces everything wrong,
but i'm happy she likes my cooking,
no one in my house really does,
prasad's too busy working,
and alia, a different person now,

"how are you all though?"
"how's little alia doing?"
"is she okay?"
an anxious flood of thoughts,
seem to spill out of her mouth,

tears come out the edges of my eyes,
filled with guilt,

she sees me crying and gives me a hug,
i'm not a very touchy person,
but i hug her back tight,
i need someone, don't i?
i deserve someone, don't i?

(no, i don't,

i didn't take care of my daughters)

"alia's in her room all the time,

or she's in mira's talking,

talking to someone,

i don't know," i confess.

"i'm not making her feel better."

idiot

you

barely

know

camila.

she gives me another hug,

"first you need to feel better,"

"and prasad, he's never at home,

when he is, he's angry, mad,

he's struggling, but i'm starting to,

almost hate him."

"is that wrong?"

words tumble out of my mouth,

it's been a year since mira's gone,

and i haven't told anyone anything since,

she stays silent and listens,

that's what i like most about camila,

she always listens.

(this is new okay?

i never knew her,

until now)

sometimes,

you get to know someone,

when,

deepest

darkest

secrets,

collect,

in front of you.

the doorbell rings again,

and i wipe my tears,

walk up to open it,

"prasad……" i say,

"you're home early."

                    "you sound like you don't want me here."
                              i turn back and glance at camila,
                              and bring him a cup of water,
                                   "enough aarthi," he says,
                              "it's enough you took care of us all,
                              we all know how well you do that,"

                    tears spill an   d he pretends,
                    he pretends h e doesn't see them,
                    he pretends h e doesn't see,
                         camil a raging,
                    he preten ds so well,
                         it hurt s so much.
                              (sha ped
                              li ke

a

b

r

o

k

e

n

heart)

"leave her alone," camila says,
"i thought you were nice."

(**spoiler v.** not nice)

i turn to her and stare,
calm down, i say with my eyes,
it's okay, i'm used to this,

"please don't come in my family matters,"
his words seem polite but the manner,
it stings like a bee sting,
she turns around to face me,

"i'm leaving aarthi, come to the potluck."

"what potluck?" prasad asks,
"doesn't she know that,
we're
broken
pieces,
that
cannot
form
anything?"
(much alone go to a social event)
i leave him there and walk to my room,
pretending to not hear.

– sometimes you need silence

(acquaintance of a princess)

"hello," i say to alia,

she walks past me,

her bag on her shoulder,

the slump of her back,

as if to go somewhere hurriedly,

"where are you going?"

she does not set the atmosphere,

girls leisurely walking,

boys talking and teasing,

as they move,

she's the only one,

moving with a purpose,

but i'm not sure if it's a good one,

                        "nowhere," she says,

but it's obvious she's lying,

i don't press further,

"don't you have chem?"

i say,

is this how our friendship,

turns out,

like a worn and severely used dress,

now too frayed?

                              "i'm heading home." she says,

                                      "i can't take this anymore,"

"i'm coming too," i say,

running off to grab my bag,

when i'm back,

i'm surprised, she hasn't left,

maybe she craves friendship,

as much as i do,

we walk out the back door,

the dozing security guard,

oblivious,

we chuckle at each other,

a smile on our faces,

after so long,

"is your mom at home?"

i ask,

knowing the answer,

                              "nah, when is she ever,"

                                          she says,

and there's a moment of normalcy,

the feeling we have in a rainbow,

of   f r i e n d s h i p,

the feeling so right,

when we reach the driveway,

we jog up to the door,

and the key fits in,

the house is empty,

smells of cleanser,

old homes,

i remember being here,

a

 year

back,

the feeling of,

 roses and play-dough,

it smelt like a home,

the carpet is tidy,

not a thing to be seen,

my home is

u n c o m f o r t a b l y   m e s s y,

      (old ciggarete burns litter the rented couch,

          paint streaks on the carpet,

          last tenant gone crazy,

          piles of clothes,

          'cuz,

      mom says we don't need a laundry bin,

          it's too e x p e n s i v e)

but at the moment,

i prefer my home, a home,

a home that maybe sometimes,

has cruel words spoken in;

(but at least we yell out our feelings)

the look on alia's eyes seems,

a welling ocean of trapped guilt,

feelings so wide,

so sticky and messy like slime,

that can't be let out onto the carpet,

"room?" i point upstairs, with a question,

                          "sure she says," smiling,
                    (spoiler vii. fake smiles always)

we're laying on the bed, the air around us,

not so light anymore,

"hey seriously though,

 what happened to your,

3rd grade crush?"

                          "oh that dumbo,"
                    she says rolling her eyes,
                       the air presses off us
                            i can breathe,

"he wasn't really
 that good looking,"
i smile,

                              "do you want me to talk
                                about your crush?"
                              she says haughtily,

"the asian dude
with glasses?"
i cover my hands,
 in my head,
"he was such a nerd,"
i say peeking through,
we laugh and then,

there's silence for a moment,
"alia, are you okay?"
i ask,
failing grades,
 silence,
the only two things,
 alia,
has been having
and doing,
ever since mira was gone,

(today seems to be april fools to me,

i'm scared she's going to say,

this isn't me now

i haven't changed,

this is a prank)

"i'm fine," she says,

her hands are tucked beneath her thighs,

i hate that i ruined this moment,

yet, a necessary question,

there's silence again,

she heads to the restroom,

without another word,

i glance around her room,

the only place in the house,

that's not spotless,

there's old clothes on the chair,

books thrown out,

but d u s t y,

a sock, comes out of the drawer,

i look at the drawer,

alia is not herself,

i think,

opening it slightly,

i shuffle to the bottom,

hoping to find nothing,

alia isn't that kind of person,

she is smart, bright,

wonderfully

sweet,

i tell myself,

she

hasn't

been

acting

like

that,

i also tell myself,

a plastic bag catches my eye.

– how can light things be so heavy?

(princess of light)

classic love story,

they said,

narrating every detail,

"mom was 21", dad says,

"dad was 21", mom says,

and the synchrony of it all,

warms your heart,

"we saw each other,

in college", says mom,

"and we hated each other,"

"i thought he was obnoxious,"

"i thought she was too girly,"

"but i remember,

we were both elected for class rep,"

"we were arguing so fiercely,

i think we just loved,

the feel of it,"

"the feel of debating,

not arguing"

dad got a smack on the hand,

"yeah kids, don't argue,"

he says in a dad voice,

we all laugh.

but it wasn't just a happy romance,

like a family drama,

oppressing mother-in-law's,

and, joyful aunts,

sceptical father-in-law's,

did not make like easy for ma,

                              (and pa as well, i guess?)

pa never got to talk with his mom,

after he married her,

the girl of his dreams,

but his sisters never lost contact,

yet he won't go to india,

not once to visit,

the loving siblings,

who had his back.

                              – he is s c a r e d

(princess of dark)

when i came back,

elaine stood there,

~~a plastic bag,~~

~~my drugs,~~

parts of me,

 in her hand,

i stared in her eye, i say,

"you don't get to say anything,"

i stare back at the deadly look,

her asian eyes dark,

"what are you doing!?"

there's a look in her eyes,

swimming between,

~~fear,~~

~~sadness,~~

anger,

~~a hurricane of feelings~~

one feeling

the knight shall not come   79

"you don't understand,

they're all gone," i say,

~~"i have only mira,"~~

("i don't have me anymore.")

      "mira! alia, mira's gone,"

     she says, tears pooling out,

      her voice gentle,

    she puts a hand on my shoulder,

"~~no,~~" i cry,
"she's in her room,
 and she'll talk to me,"

    "alia, i think you need some help,"

     "i'm real, mira's not,"

     "please don't do this,"

   she says when i crumple up on the floor,

      sobbing,

she steps over me to the restroom,

throws the pills in the toilet,

and ~~flushes~~,

no, she shall not

again and again,

"~~damn thing,~~" ~~she says,~~
"~~it's not going in!~~"

she comes out and sit by my sobbing side,

"look, mira was wonderful,
whoever is haunting you,
that's not her."
"~~you are haunting yourself~~"

i sob harder,
everything is being taken away,
mom and dad,
now mira and my best friend,
~~its funny~~
~~its sad,~~
~~i'm mad~~
all of the above,
how things never last,

no matter how hard you try.

"mira

is

breathing

and

~~dancing~~

and

living"

i still yell defiantly,

"please leave,"

i have to push her away,

if she stays,

she'll dispose of that little,

~~plastic bag.~~

part of me?

    – i'm just ~~confused..~~ no.. i don't know.

(royal acquaintance turned duchess)

she hangs on to a thread,

a thread connecting her,

to herself,

i worry for her,

my brows wrinkle,

as i stare at the bright girl,

on the floor weeping,

she looks at me,

almost with hate in her eyes,

like i'm taking everything away,

i'm not taking anything away,

i'm trying to give her,

her

 life

back,

"i'm

not

leaving,"

i say defiant,

"i'll

stay

here

with

you

for

as

long,

as

i

need

to

stay,"

she is sad.

"don't tell ma, please,"

(spoiler alert.. *d o n ' t   t e l l   m a?*)

"i'm telling her."

she wipes her tears away and says,
"she already knows,"

"what!?"
alia's ma,
is sweet and caring,
like the touch of a butterfly,
protective like the ocean,
she's dedicated to her work,
but she cares,
i stay silent,
words don't flow,
like they had been

"elaine," she looks up at me,
"thank you."

"thank you for what?" i ask,
but there is a tight grip on my throat,
and perhaps this confirmation was,
exactly what i needed,
acknowledgement of the fact,

that i've been by her side,

for the past few months,

no matter how shit,

she acts.

she doesn't respond,

she knows that i k n o w.

        – not awkward silence. it's the needed
        silence of friendship.

(queen)

(**spoiler viii**. a damsel in distress now.)

i remember when alia was in school,

i was stuck at home,

with a frenzy of a fever,

but my hands wouldn't stop itching,

my

eyes

kept

looking

at

her

door,

alia was not herself,

her words flow sweetly.

like honey dripping out of,

a honeycomb,

they're not angry like a herd,

stampeding out of her mouth,

she radiates success,

or hard work,

not the report cards,

she rips into the trash.

that was the day,

i searched her room,

like i'd never,

have a c h a n c e to see her again,

(i knew her silent mom,

couldn't reprimand her,

after leaving her for months,

of parenting herself,

but i searched all the same,

knowing that my findings,

would gnaw at my soul

more than bring a change)

please, i murmured,

please

 don't

let

me

fail

as

a

mother,

but mostly,

please don't trap alia,

i want her to be happy,

and confident,

a young women proud,

of her achievements.

my hands frayed violently,

as i looked through her clothes,

tears streaming down my face,

i felt out of control,

a hurricane of thoughts,

of worries flooding my head,

but i didn't stop,

until the carpet was littered with,

clothes and salt,

pouring out of my eyes.

my once itching hand,

drooping with the weight,

of plastic.

now the silence of pain.

(princess of light)

she stays by your side,

but you know it's,

getting dark outside,

you know mom will come,

silent downstairs,

never checking on you,

she won't say hi,

>(and elaine will,
>
>elaine will,
>
>hate your ~~ma,~~
>
>your ~~sweet~~ mom)

and then dad will come,

a bucket full of,

sharp daggers,

>words he twists into weaponry,

when did he become like this?

you question,

when did dad's kiss,

stop itching you with,

sharp stubble?

when did his embrace,

stop feeling safe?

when did conversation,

stop feeling so light?

he might not talk to you,

now,

 but he will attack ma,

ma,

who doesn't know,

i'm right here,

before your eyes,

melancholically,

ma whose words droop,

heavy with the weight of,

loss and pain,

failure and sadness,

and you think,

she's worse off than you.

you don't understand that dad blames not you,

but ma, for losing both you and me,

he casts a look, filled with hatred,

an emotion that masks sadness, ever so well,

but maybe, just maybe,

he thinks he's lost us all,

and he doesn't know how to,

stop.

> – you are not a failure until you start
> blaming others for your mistakes

(the duchess)

alia's dead eyes look at me,

conveying a bit more,

than death,

it's clear she's itching,

for me to exit,

and at this point,

my legs want to jump,

up and run out,

of this cursed house,

to a better hell,

(hell it is,

but a better one)

you

want

to

do

something

you can't

except listen,

but you can't listen,

if the words don't flow out,

the knight shall not come   93

of her mouth,

her mouth stays shut,

and your friendship almost feels,

~~a little bit broken.~~

~~broken.~~

torn,

like the wings of a butterfly.

"bye," she says, when i stand up,

"no, i wasn't planning on leaving," i say,

"i needed to use the restroom,"

she eyes me,

as if to say,

it's best for both of us,

"i don't think you'll,

like my house,

when they all,

reach the house,"

she says finally,

after a long pause,

her voice breaking,

i don't like it now,

i think,

to myself

i know she doesn't want me to stay,

but i feel

guilty.

guilty.

for leaving her alone.

at home,

as ma expects me,

to race through homework,

i lay,

on the bed,

brows furrowed,

– what could i do?

(princess of dark)

the world spins on its axis,

ma and dad

come

 home

 at

the

same time,

a fierce wording of arguments,

      "you can't just blame me,"

      ma says,

      "you're just as much to blame"

      there's tears oozing out of her eyes,

      out of anger,

      not the silent tears,

      of sadness,

"you ruined us,"

"it's you're oversight that got us here,"

he throws words without any,

true meaning,

                              "shut up!"

                         ma says loudly,

                         turning around,

that's when i hear the sharp sound,

          a ringing sound,

                    of tight skin touching,

                         supple skin,

                              a sharp scream,

i imagine,

          eyes staring at eyes,

                    ma's eyes daggering,

but that's probably not true,

                    ma's hand probably,

                         goes to her cheek,

and she turns away,

i want her to say,,

                    "i'm done with you."

but there's only,

the soft sound,

of footsteps after that,

an hour later,

i hear vent up emotions,

pouring out of ma,

"i'm divorcing you,"

she screams,

her voice loud and shrill,

why does a spark of joy,

rise up my heart?

– joy is nothing to ever, ever, feel guilty about.

(queen)

(spoiler ix. now a f e m a l e   m o n a r c h)

pain blackened my eyes,

for a few seconds,

i bent down,

and he left me there,

on the floor,

as much as i want to,

pick up the remains,

the lost puzzlc pieces,

are far too many,

to make any kind of picture,

yet i stay silent,

i don't tell him a word,

i go to the kitchen and start chopping onion,

masking the tears flowing out of my eyes,

i wish for alia,

her old self would run down,

tell me what to do,

tell me he's not worth it,

but no footsteps are heard,

when i cut my finger,

raw and deep,

i know i don't want pain,

a sound comes out of me,

that even i don't expect,

"i'm divorcing you,"

i scream,

loudly,

and he just stares at my face,

scared of a woman's,

     burning hot anger,

        he walks out the door,

           and i know he won't be back.

      – sometimes people need to leave, or you
      need to leave them. period (3rd one)

(duchess)

(spoiler x. is there a duke?)

i'm at the old brick wall,

behind the school,

where me and alia,

used to escape,

we'd sit and eat lunch,

under the shade,

of red-hot brick,

we'd look and laugh,

eat and cry,

everything happened here,

alia's not here today,

she's probably in the library,

pouring over a textbook,

staining the ink,

with hot tears.

(don't laugh)

she's avoiding me,

like i'm a monster,

one with horns,

i don't look for her either,

                              don't know what to do,

don't know what to say,

i can't force her to,

be better,

do better,

get better;

unless she actually,

wants to.

a boy, brown hair,

blue eyes,

walks up to me,

i find myself smiling,

e l e m e n t a r y s c h o o l,

images of him,

in every girl's mind,

                              "i'm sorry," he says,

and i don't think about alia,
for a moment,
i think about the way his words,
roll out of his mouth,
the way he moves,
i shake myself,
"why?"
i ask,

> "i
> gave
> it
> to
> her."
> he says,
> his words pool out,
> a puddle when you walk,
> out
> of the swimming pool,
> and you turn cold,
> the air evaporating on your skin.

but bubbling hot anger,
does not rise up into me,
i'm not mad at alia,
nor am i at cameron,

people
make
mistakes
sometimes,
he got out of it,
alia will too,
"okay." i speak.

(there
is
nothing
else
to
say)

and there's tears in my eyes.
alia isn't by my side that day,
cameron,
waits for the tears,
to stop flowing.
why does my heart beat,
just a little bit faster?

– love is a thing with f e a t h e r s. it is not
love yet. maybe forgiveness.

(princess of dark)

i'm gripping the wheel,
    knuckles white,
        fingers red,
why am i here again?
yes mira,
i look out the car,
see the smile on,
her face,

        "please take the car,
          alia,
        i'm going to miss,
        the magic show,"
         she gestures,
      at the open garage door,
         as she hops in,
         the front seat,
      seems almost scripted;

"sure," i say,
but my mouth feels dry,

and it feels,

like a red ant's,

on my lip biting,

but it's probably,

myself,

        why am i so scared?

i press the pedal,

and i hear a honk,

images swirl before,

my eyes.

it's me,

      pressing the button,

         the truck swerves,

         but it doesn't stop,

           i brace the wheel,

            knuckles tight,

"mira!"

i scream,

                  as i feel the jerk,

                    the sound,

                          i   see   blood on my elbow,

p
 o
u
    r
        i
    n
g

i don't think about the pain,

i scream,

"mira,"

she lays on the floor,

gasping,

her head on the screen,

almost laying on the glass,

her necks at an edge,

blood pools down her ribs,
                    "you'll
                      be
                     fine,"

i mutter,

panic in my raspy voice,

as my eyes go shut.

the car stays in the garage.

spoiler xi. mira is dead

spoiler xii. the princess does not need a knight in shining armour to save her

spoiler xiii. she needs herself

spoiler xiv. her story is hers to write.

imagine it however you would like.

    – hope is a thing with f e a t h e r s and i
    hope you'll have some.

(acknowledgements)

i.   my mom, excited to know about the latest developments and who read this countless times.

ii. mr. mrithyunjay, my english teacher, who made english more fun than i thought it could be.

iii. my dad, who has always been there for me.

iv. books, all the authors who poured their soul out on paper for me to read. i hope i can do that one day.

v.   samaira, who enchanted me with her words and has been a wonderful friend.

vi. shriya for being funny and just as interested in the outcome of the book, as i was.